For my children with thanks —
    K. H.

For Brady Jane —
    T. K.

Text copyright © 1999 by Kathy Henderson
Illustrations copyright © 1999 by Tony Kerins

All rights reserved.

First U.S. edition 1999

Library of Congress Cataloging-in-Publication Data

Henderson, Kathy, date.
The baby dances / Kathy Henderson ; illustrated by Tony Kerins.—1st U.S. ed.
p.   cm.
Summary: Recounts the development of a baby, from birth
to rolling over, crawling, standing, and finally walking.
ISBN 0-7636-0374-0
[1. Babies—Fiction. 2. Growth—Fiction.] I. Kerins, Tony, ill.   II. Title.
PZ7.H3805Bab   1998
[E]—dc21   98-23596

10 9 8 7 6 5 4 3 2

Printed in Hong Kong

This book was typeset in Weiss.
The pictures were done in chalk pastels.

Candlewick Press
2067 Massachusetts Avenue
Cambridge, Massachusetts 02140

The
BABY DANCES

Kathy Henderson

illustrated by
Tony Kerins

CANDLEWICK PRESS
CAMBRIDGE, MASSACHUSETTS

The baby's born.
The baby's born.

In the middle of winter

and a windy, rattling, late rainstorm

she has her first warm hug

in her father's arms . . .

look, the baby's born!

The baby sleeps.
The baby sleeps.

And the pale sun reaches

the windowsill,

where everything is still

in a room full of flowers,

and the baby sleeps for hours.

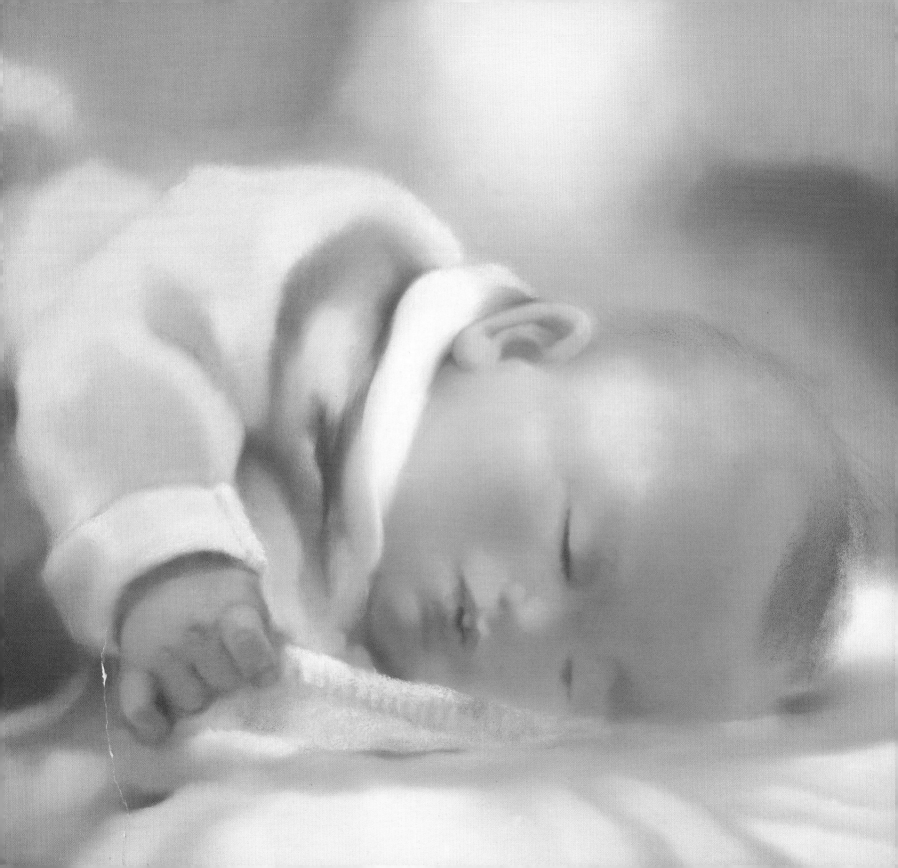

The baby's smiling.
The baby's smiling.

Lying on her back

with the spring sun shining,

riding by the blossom

and the faces passing,

now the baby's smiling.

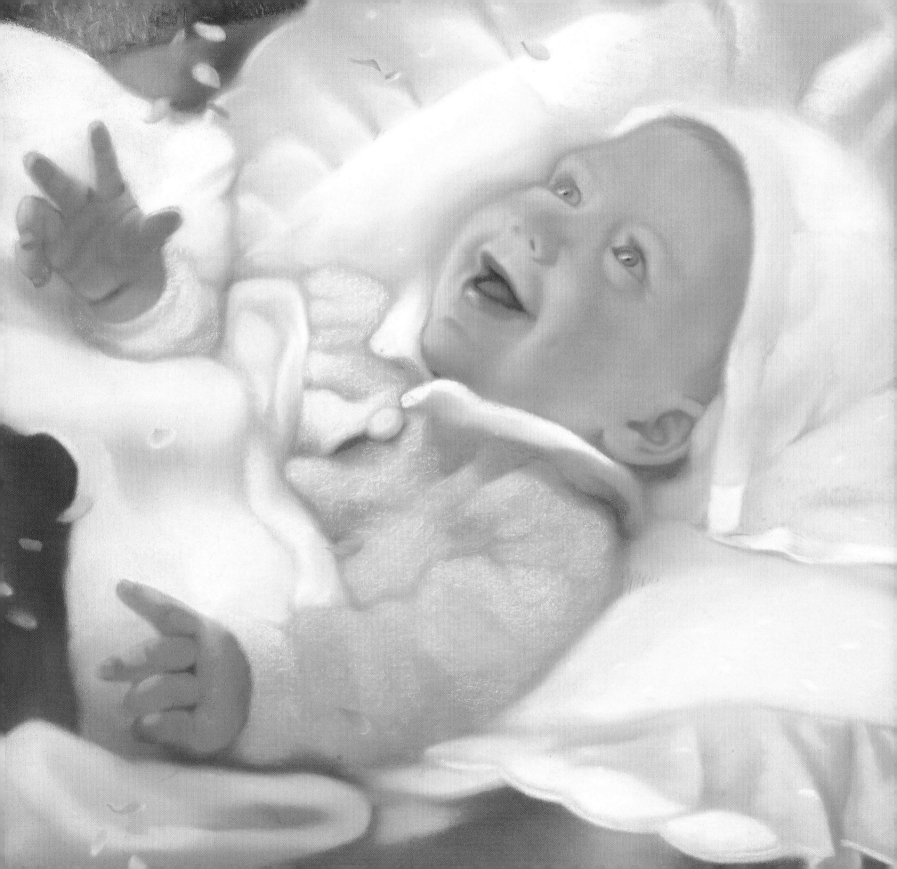

The baby rolls.
The baby rolls.

On her rug in the grass

she tips the whole world up,

with a kick and a wriggle

and a handful of clover . . .

the baby rolls herself over.

The baby sits.
The baby sits

with a cushion there to catch her

'cause she sways and leans

and wobbles a bit.

She waves her hands at shadows,

and her sun hat tips,

but the baby sits.

The baby crawls.
The baby crawls.

From sprawling on the rug

now she rocks on all fours,

and reaching out her hand

as the first dry leaf

of autumn falls . . .

the baby crawls.

The baby stands.
The baby stands

like a tightrope walker

in the gusty wind.

For a long split second

she lifts her hands

and all on her own

the baby stands.

The baby walks.
The baby walks.

By the warmth of the fire

while the winter beats outside,

she takes her first lurching steps,

reaches out . . .

staggers . . . prances . . .

and safe in her brother's arms,

the baby dances!